Mary's Song

Written by
Lee Bennett Hopkins

Illustrated by
Stephen Alcorn

Eerdmans Books for Young Readers
Grand Rapids, Michigan • Cambridge, U.K.

To my sister Donna Lea Venturi —
for the lifetime songs
we sang together.
— *L.B.H.*

For Nonna Maria, aka Nonna Badia.
— *S.A.*

Text © 2012 Lee Bennett Hopkins
Illustrations © 2012 Stephen Alcorn

Published in 2012 by Eerdmans Books for Young Readers,
an imprint of Wm. B. Eerdmans Publishing Co.
2140 Oak Industrial Dr. NE
Grand Rapids, Michigan 49505
P.O. Box 163, Cambridge CB3 9PU U.K.

www.eerdmans.com/youngreaders

Manufactured at Tien Wah Press
in Singapore in March 2012, first printing

12 13 14 15 16 17 18 19   8 7 6 5 4 3 2 1

Library of Congress Cataloging-in-Publication Data

Hopkins, Lee Bennett.
Mary's song / by Lee Bennett Hopkins; illustrated by Stephen Alcorn.
p. cm.
Summary: In the stillness of a Bethlehem stable, after the shepherds and animals leave,
Mary sings a lullaby to her newborn son, enjoying the wonder and awe of his birth and pondering what his life will bring.
ISBN 978-0-8028-5397-4 (alk. paper)
1. Mary, Blessed Virgin, Saint — Juvenile fiction. 2. Jesus Christ — Nativity — Juvenile fiction.
[1. Mary, Blessed Virgin, Saint — Fiction. 2. Jesus Christ — Nativity — Fiction.]
I. Alcorn, Stephen, ill. II. Title.
PZ7.H7754Mar 2012
[E] — dc23
2011035890

The illustrations were rendered in mixed-media on ivory paper.
The type was set in Cheltenham.

It wasn't the angel Gabriel.

His voice was so quiet-soft when he whispered:

Thou shalt bring forth a son,

and shalt call his name Jesus.

He shall be great, and shall be called

the Son of the Highest;

and of his kingdom there shall be no end.

It wasn't the trip to Bethlehem.
Joseph and I were weary — tired.
There wasn't even a bray uttered
from the burdened donkey.

It didn't start the moment he was born.
There was silence with just Joseph,
   me, and my babe wrapped
   in swaddling clothes, lying so peacefully
   in a manger.

It began suddenly.

First were mumblings from simple shepherds —

who came from nearby fields,

who were told by an angel:

Today a Savior is born unto you,
and he is Christ the Lord.

They knew, at once, they had to see him.

Then it was the animals — each peaceful, respectful,
yet they could not contain the gladness felt
as they gazed on him in reverence.

Sheep bleated.

Donkeys brayed and brayed.

Horses neighed and neighed.

Cattle were lowing.

Crickets chirped.

Doves were coo-coo-ing.

Mice squeaked and squealed
as they excitedly rustled through
dry straw covering the old barn floor.

I even thought I heard a whisper
from spider above the manger,
spinning her web —
though I know what silent spinners
spiders are.

Noises didn't bother my babe.
They did me.
I longed to be alone with him.

At last, one by one,
each shepherd,
each animal left the barn.
Except spider, whose huge, commanding web
shone down like the brightest
crystallized star I had ever seen.

The barn was quiet now.

Still.

No more voices.

No more

braying, bleating,

neighing, lowing,

chirping, coo-coo-ing,

squeaking, squealing.

Only quiet now.

Quiet.

Holding him cradled in my arms,
I rock back and forth,
forth and back,
softly humming my mother-song.

I wonder what will become of him,
my sweet innocent babe.

As I
rock back and forth,
forth and back,
he looks up at me and smiles.

I look up at the web.

Spider seems to be humming a mother-song

to her newborn, too.

Awe
Wonder

Today —
birth of him.

My
baby
boy.